Robin Muller

13 Ghosts of Halloween

illustrated by
Patricia Storms

Kane Miller
A DIVISION OF EDC PUBLISHING

To Khalen Perkins, with *howls*
and *shrieks* and candy
bags full of Happy Halloween.
– R.M.

For my Guido.
– P.S.

First American Edition 2009
by Kane Miller, A Division of EDC Publishing
Tulsa, Oklahoma

First published by Scholastic Canada Ltd. in 2007
Text copyright © 2007 by Robin Muller
Illustrations copyright © 2007 by Patricia Storms

Library of Congress Control Number: 2009922721
Printed and bound in China by Regent Publishing Services Ltd.
1 2 3 4 5 6 7 8 9 10
ISBN: 978-1-935279-14-3

On the first stroke of midnight
Oh, nothing frightens me!
Not a vulture in a dead tree.

On the second stroke of midnight
Oh, nothing frightens me!
Not two shrunken heads
Or a vulture in a dead tree.

On the third stroke of midnight
Oh, nothing frightens me!
Not three black cats
Two shrunken heads
Or a vulture in a dead tree.

On the fourth stroke of midnight
Oh, nothing frightens me!
Not four darting bats
Three black cats
Two shrunken heads
Or a vulture in a dead tree.

On the fifth stroke of midnight
No, nothing frightens me!
Not five bogeymen

Four darting bats
Three black cats
Two shrunken heads
Or a vulture in a dead tree.

On the sixth stroke of midnight
Oh, nothing frightens me!
Not six pumpkins grinning
Five bogeymen

Four darting bats
Three black cats
Two shrunken heads
Or a vulture in a dead tree.

On the seventh stroke of midnight
Oh, nothing frightens me!
Not seven spiders spinning
Six pumpkins grinning
Five bogeymen
Four darting bats
Three black cats
Two shrunken heads
Or a vulture in a dead tree.

On the eighth stroke of midnight
Oh, nothing frightens me!
Not eight mummies moaning
Seven spiders spinning
Six pumpkins grinning
Five bogeymen
Four darting bats
Three black cats
Two shrunken heads
Or a vulture in a dead tree.

On the ninth stroke of midnight
Oh, nothing frightens me!
Not nine witches cackling
Eight mummies moaning
Seven spiders spinning
Six pumpkins grinning
Five bogeymen

Four darting bats
Three black cats
Two shrunken heads
Or a vulture in a dead tree.

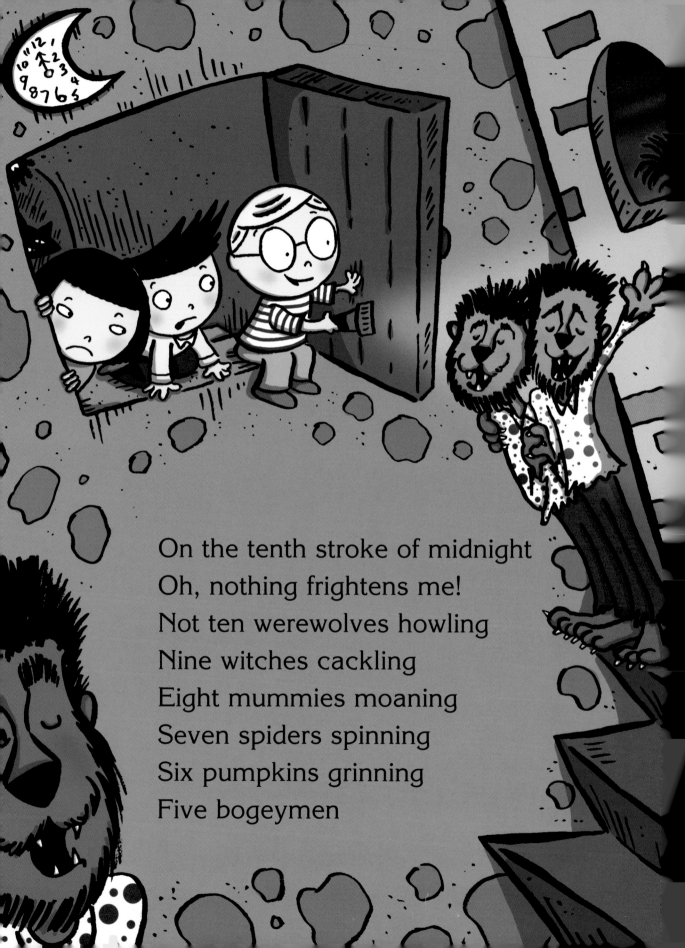

On the tenth stroke of midnight
Oh, nothing frightens me!
Not ten werewolves howling
Nine witches cackling
Eight mummies moaning
Seven spiders spinning
Six pumpkins grinning
Five bogeymen

Four darting bats
Three black cats
Two shrunken heads
Or a vulture in a dead tree.

On the eleventh stroke of midnight
Oh, nothing frightens me!
Not eleven goblins giggling
Ten werewolves howling
Nine witches cackling
Eight mummies moaning
Seven spiders spinning
Six pumpkins grinning
Five bogeymen
Four darting bats
Three black cats
Two shrunken heads
Or a vulture in a dead tree.

On the twelfth stroke of midnight
Oh, nothing frightens me!
Not twelve vampires rising
Eleven goblins giggling
Ten werewolves howling
Nine witches cackling
Eight mummies moaning
Seven spiders spinning
Six pumpkins grinning
Five bogeymen
Four darting bats
Three black cats
Two shrunken heads
Or a vulture in a dead tree.

On the **thirteenth** stroke of midnight
Yes, something frightened me . . .

a ghost!